Bertie the Bouncy Beachball

by Mandy Woolf

Illustrated by Elmira Georgieva

Dedicated to

My Mummy who was beautiful
inside and out.

Bertie lives on a wonky, old shelf
squashed between toys.

Each morning as the sun rises,
the toys gather around.

Then at eight o'clock sharp, the door opens
wide and a stampede of feet rush in.

Swoosh

Everyone stays very still... especially Bertie.
He holds his breath as hands dive in.
"Pick me," mutters Bertie.

Then the room grows silent once more.
Bertie looks around.

Spade is exercising, Sandcastle is snoring
and Green Bucket is collecting shapes.

"Next time," he whispers.

At lunchtime, the door bangs open again, and children rush in.
They move towards him, and Bertie holds his breath.

Spade, are you there?

Green Bucket,
can you hear me?

Sandcastle,
shall we play cards?

But everyone has gone.
Everyone apart from Bertie.

"Now I understand," he whispers.

"I'm too patchy... My colour has faded...

I bump instead of roll..."

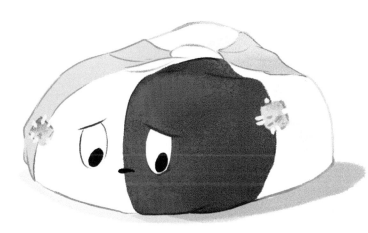

Bertie slumps down.
"I probably can't even bounce anymore."

Loud voices startle him as the door opens again.
"There's not much left," puffs Grandpa Nathan.

"Lets' take this one!" squeals Rosie.

"It's a bit... shabby," moans Esther.

"That doesn't mean
it won't be fun," replies Rosie.

Bertie is dizzy with excitment.
"Really, you want ME? ... are you sure?
I'm more of a BUMPER than a roller.

I'm not..." but Bertie is already outside.

What if he disappoints everyone?

Bertie tries hard to bounce,
but rolls right into Sandcastle.
"Sorry!" he cries.

"You can do it, Bertie. Just try bending your knees," encourages Sandcastle. So, he does and....

Bounce, bounce,
BOUNCE!

Rosie and Esther
clap with joy.

"See I told you it would be fun!" cries Rosie.

Bertie bounces higher and higher and .... HIGHER!

Suddenly,
all eyes are on Bertie.

"Can we join?"
And Bertie's smile is GLORIOUS!

Bertie bounces on knees
and rolls through legs.

He swoops through the air
and plays catch.

He bounces and bounces
and BOUNCES!

Bertie tries to savour every wonderful moment.
But all too soon the day ends,

and it is time for him to return
to the wonky old shelf.

As his new friends gently close the door behind them,
Bertie smiles as everyone agrees that he really is the
BOUNCIEST beachball that they have ever played with!

DISCUSSION FOR CHILDREN, PARENTS AND TEACHERS.

1. Where does Bertie live?

2. What happens at 8 o'clock sharp?

3. Who is collecting shapes?

4. Why is Bertie sad?

5. How does that make you feel?

6. Why do you think it makes you feel that way?

7. How could you help Bertie feel better?

8. Who gives Bertie a chance?

9. Why is Bertie worried?

10. Have you ever been worried?

11. What advice does sandcastle give?

12. What happens to Bertie's Bounce?

13. What do Bertie's new friends all agree on?